My Wiggly Smile

Olive's Stubborn Little Tooth

Written by Dr. Amira May Woodruff

Artwork by Toby Mikle

D1396827

© 2018 AMW Solutions, All Rights Reserved

"Olive...It's time to get up," says Mom.
"First day of kindergarten, here I come!" squeals Olive.

At breakfast, Olive's brother Bryce tattles,
"Mom, Olive has her fingers in her mouth."

"I can't stop wiggling my tooth.
Why won't it come out?" Olive wonders.

"Hi, what's your name?"
Olive asks the boy sitting next to her in class.

"Hi, I'm Wilson Spee," he whispers back.

"And I'm Jordan Christensen," says a girl.

"Nice to meet you both, I'm —"

Just then, Olive is cut off by their teacher's roll call. "Olive Carabelli."

"That's me!" Olive exclaims.

"You've already lost a tooth?" asks Olive admiringly when she sees that Jordan has a space between her bottom teeth.

"Yes, it came out a few days ago," Jordan says proudly. "I was so excited to finally color my first tooth missing in the *My Wiggly Smile* book."

Olive starts, "What is —"

"Okay, everyone. Welcome to your first day of kindergarten!" announces Ms. Dot.

The school day is so busy that Olive doesn't get to ask Jordan what she was talking about.

At the end of the day, Ms. Dot dismisses the class and Olive rushes to meet Bryce at the school's front door. "Hi Bryce, how was second grade?" Olive asks while wiggling her tooth with her tongue.

"I won a spelling bee," Bryce boasts.

"Excellent," yells Olive, ready for a high-five.

Bryce glances at the older kids nearby and settles for a secret low-five. Olive smiles and slaps it hard, not noticing a thing.

"Dad, I LOVE kindergarten! I made a new friend. Her name is Jordan. Bryce won a spelling bee," Olive says quickly.

"I'm so proud of the both of you!" Dad says.

Noticing Olive still wiggling her tooth, Dad reaches into a bag. "I have something for you."

"Wow, Dad! Jordan said she has this *My Wiggly Smile* book. I didn't know what she was talking about," says Olive.

"Well now you have it too, Olive. We have a couple of things to do this afternoon. First we're going to stop by Uncle Mike and Aunt Claire's house to drop off Wyatt's birthday present. Then Mom's going to meet us at the dentist," says Dad.

"Yay, I get to see Wyatt. He's my favorite cousin in the whole wide world!" Olive squeals. She flips through her new book and checks out the tooth holder necklace.

"Happy birthday!" Olive shouts as Wyatt opens the front door.

"How old are you now?" asks Dad.

"I'm thirteen—finally a teenager," Wyatt says proudly as Bryce hands Wyatt his present.

"Does somebody have a loose tooth?" Wyatt
asks, noticing Olive's *My Wiggly Smile* book.

"Yes!" Olive says frustrated. "I've been wiggling
it all day and it won't budge!"

"I want to show you something," says Wyatt.
"Follow me."

"I lost the last of my twenty baby teeth this summer," says Wyatt.

"Does that mean the tooth fairy visited you twenty times?" gasps Olive.

"Yes, she did," says Wyatt.

"You forgot to color in your last tooth on
the tooth chart. Can I do it for you?"
asks Olive as she looks at
her cousin's book.

"Sure," says Wyatt.

"Olive, time to go to the dentist,"
calls Dad.

In the waiting room at the dental office,
Olive sits on Mom's lap. She shows
off her new book and tooth holder necklace.

"Olive Carabelli?" calls the dental assistant
when it's Olive's turn to see
the dentist.

"Well, Olive, you do have a very loose tooth," says Dr. May. "Your mom said that you can wait for it to fall out by itself or I can help wiggle it out today."

Olive says, "Wiggle it out today! I want the tooth fairy to come tonight!"

"Okay, let me get a closer look," says Dr. May. "All you have to do is open wide and keep your hands on your belly."

Olive asks, "Dr. May, will this hurt?"

Dr. May asks, "Did you bring your tooth holder necklace?"

"Yes," says Olive, "it's right here."

"Will you show me which tooth I lost today,
so I can color it in my book?" asks Olive.

"You lost tooth letter O," says Dr. May, pointing to
the page. "Here is a crayon for you to color it in."

"O for Olive!" says Olive.

"Why do baby teeth fall out?" asks Olive.

"A baby tooth falls out because your grown-up tooth is trying to come in and pushes it out," explains Dr. May. "Olive, you were a good listener today. You may pick a toy out of the toy chest."

When they get home, Olive and Bryce
play football in the backyard.

After a while, Dad calls, "Come in and wash up. It's time for dinner."

"Hi Grandpa! Hi Grandma!" exclaims Olive.
"Are you having dinner with us?"

"Yes we are, my dear," says Grandpa.

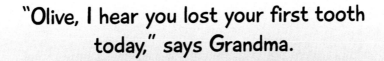

"Olive, I hear you lost your first tooth today," says Grandma.

"Yes I did," says Olive. "I can't wait for the tooth fairy tonight!"

"Okay, you two, it is bedtime,"
says Mom later that night.

Olive asks, "Grandpa, will you tuck me in?"

"Of course I will," says Grandpa.
"Go get ready for bed. I will be there in a
few minutes."

While tucking Olive in, Grandpa says,
"Guess what. I still have one of my
baby teeth."

"But Grandpa, you're old!" exclaims Olive.

"Do you remember that a baby tooth falls out when the
grown-up tooth grows and pushes it out?"
asks Grandpa.

"Yes," responds Olive.

"One of my grown-up teeth never grew,
so the baby tooth is still there,"
says Grandpa.

"Wow!" says Olive.

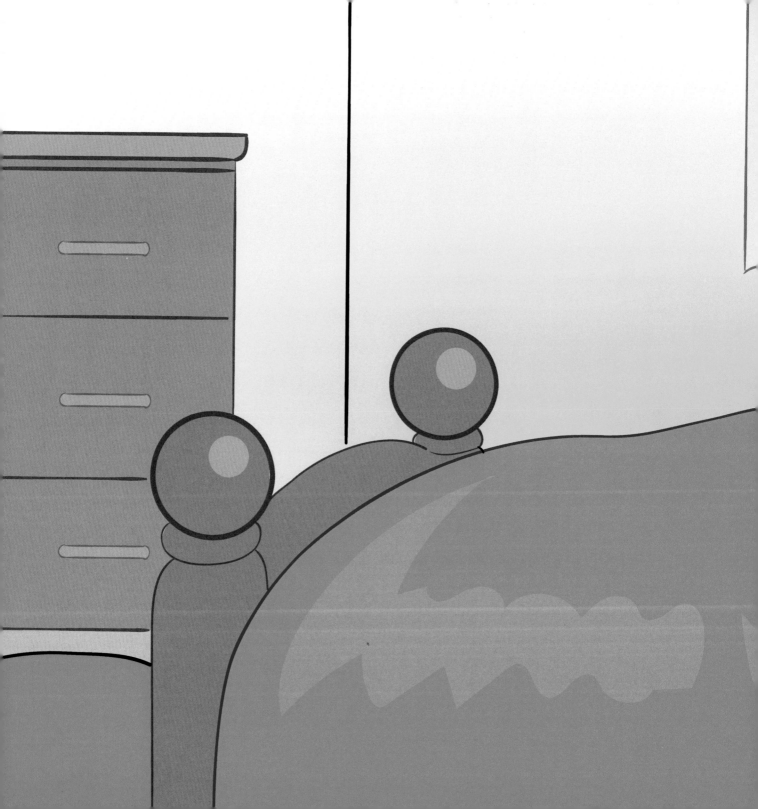

"Mom! Dad!

The tooth fairy was here!"

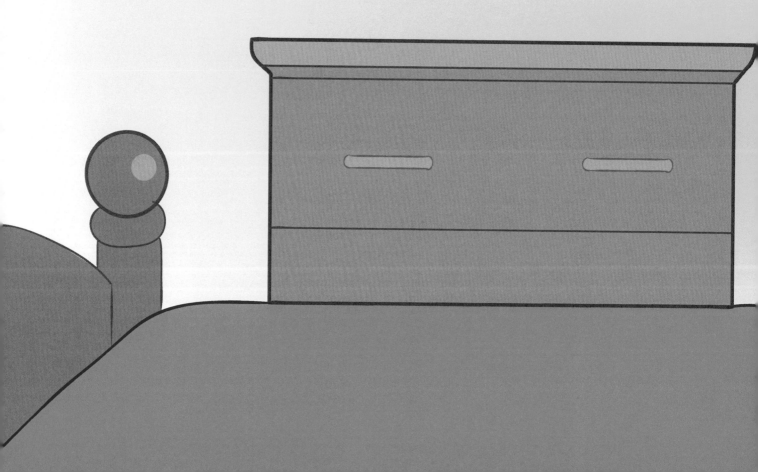

The Age Baby Teeth Fall Out

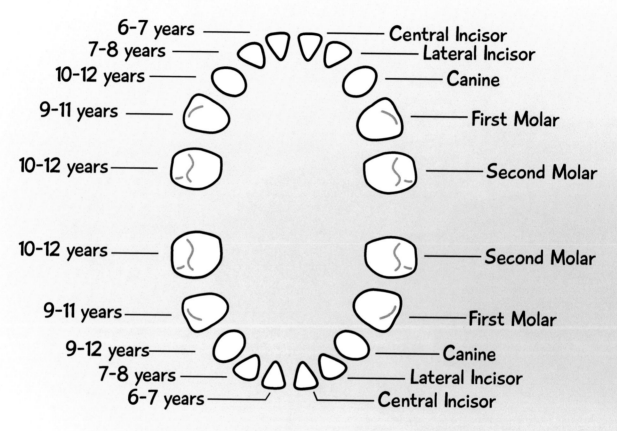

6-7 years — Central Incisor
7-8 years — Lateral Incisor
10-12 years — Canine
9-11 years — First Molar
10-12 years — Second Molar

10-12 years — Second Molar
9-11 years — First Molar
9-12 years — Canine
7-8 years — Lateral Incisor
6-7 years — Central Incisor

Everyone's mouth is different.
If your teeth fall out a little sooner or later than expected, that is okay.

This Wiggly Smile Belongs to

_____

(write your name here)

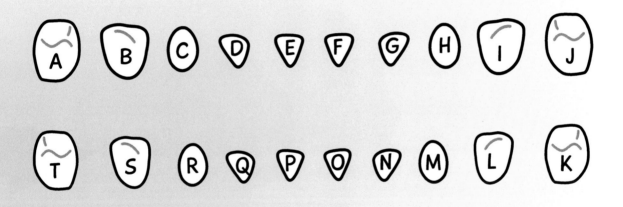

Each baby tooth is named with a letter of the alphabet. When you lose a tooth, color it in on your chart. Make sure to confirm which tooth you lost with your dentist.

68661907R00024

Made in the USA
Middletown, DE
31 March 2018